10   9   8   7   6

British Library Cataloguing in Publication Data available.

ISBN 978 1 84270 426 4

Tadpole's Promise

Jeanne Willis

Tony Ross

Ⓐ

Andersen Press
London

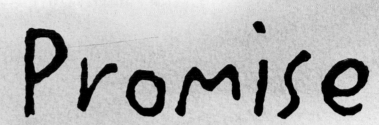

Where the willow meets the water
a tadpole met a caterpillar.
They gazed into each other's tiny eyes . . .

. . . and fell in love.
She was his beautiful rainbow,

and he was her shiny black pearl.
"I love everything about you,"
said the tadpole.

"I love everything about you," said the caterpillar. "Promise you'll never change."

"I promise," he said.

But as sure as the weather changes,
the tadpole could not keep his promise.
Next time they met, he had grown two legs.

"You've broken your promise,"
                            said the caterpillar.

"Forgive me," begged the tadpole.
"I couldn't help it. I don't want these legs . . .

All I want is my beautiful rainbow."

"All I want is my shiny black pearl.
Promise me you'll never change,"
said the caterpillar.

"I promise," he said.

But as sure as the seasons change,
the next time they met –
he had grown arms.

"That's twice you've broken your promise," cried the caterpillar.

"Forgive me," begged the tadpole. "I could not help it.
I do not want these arms . . .

All I want is my beautiful rainbow."

"And all I want is my shiny black pearl.
I will give you one last chance,"
said the caterpillar.

But as surely as the world changes,
   the tadpole could not keep his promise.
   The next time they met –

                         he had no tail.

"You have broken your promise three times,
and now you have broken my heart,"
said the caterpillar.

"But you are my beautiful rainbow," said the tadpole.

"Yes, but you are not my shiny black pearl. Goodbye."

She crawled up the willow branch, and cried herself to sleep.

One warm moonlit night,
she woke up.
The sky had changed,
The trees had changed.
Everything had changed . . .

. . . except for her love for the tadpole.
Even though he'd broken his promise,
she decided to forgive him.

She dried her wings
and fluttered down to look for him.

Where the willow meets the water,
a frog was sitting on a lily pad.

"Excuse me," she said.
"Have you seen my shiny black . . ."

But faster than she could say 'pearl',
the frog leapt up and swallowed her,

in one great gulp.

And there he waits . . .

. . . thinking fondly of his beautiful rainbow . . .

. . . wondering where she went.

THE END

Tadpole's Promise